How to Survive Middle School

The Guide to Survive

Anastasia L. Douglas

ISBN 978-1-0980-1406-3 (paperback)
ISBN 978-1-0980-1407-0 (digital)

Christian Faith Publishing, Inc.
832 Park Avenue
Meadville, PA 16335
www.christianfaithpublishing.com

Printed in the United States of America

Dedication

This book is dedicated to my Lord and Saviour Jesus Christ for putting it in my heart to write this book. Also to my parents Melvin and Angela Douglas who were always there for me when I was upset or having a hard time. My loving/crazy sisters Jasmine and Sherron, my brother-in-law Maurice, and my niece Adara who listened to and supported me. A great woman and mentor Ms. Evans for helping me show the world my talent, for seeing the best in me, and being a great mentor. My middle school ELA teachers, Mrs. Karen McInnis, Mrs. Natalie Chaisson, and Ms. Sarah McMillan "Thank you guys so much for teaching me. Without the knowledge in English this wouldn't even be a book. Lastly but never forgotten to every child who has ever been bullied, and for every child who goes through middle school this is especially dedicated to you because you were my inspiration to write this.

Contents

Introduction

Middle school is an interesting place. You meet new people and see many different things. Most seventh and eighth graders say they're ready for high school. Well, not everyone is prepared for that stage of their life. Most kids who start high school say it is way different from middle school, and let me just say I believe them. In life, there's almost a guide for everything, but has anyone given you a guide for middle school? Lucky for you, I'm here to help with the situation you might be in. Read my advice and experiences on getting ready and surviving middle school. I guarantee it will help you with this crazy adventure that you will go on or already experiencing. So lets get started.

Chapter 1

The First Day

The first day can be a big mess. Usually, people stress over what they're going to wear or who they're going to talk to. If you're like me, you stress over your schedule. I can remember my first day. It wasn't the best of all the first days I've had so far in my life. Yes, you're going to be nervous and very scared to take that first step. That's fine; lots of people are like that on their first day. Just remember to take a deep breath and go for it.

Getting out of the car, your hands start to sweat, and you see different people you don't know. Don't be afraid to show people who you are. Never be that person who just hides behind their clothes or is distant from other people. It's perfectly fine to be a little shy, but don't be shy all the time.

Walk into the school with confidence. Keep that swag with you to show people who they're messing with.

Of course, you have to find what classes you have to go to. So you get your brand new schedule. Since this is all new, you have absolutely nowhere to go.

Never back down from asking for help. You might be thinking people will think you're a weirdo and a strange kid if you ask. From my personal experience, they'll help you out so much. Always greet them with a smile, and just ask for directions. Literally, it's that easy. I can't stress that enough.

The person you asked helps give you directions to your classroom. This is where it's hard for some kids. Where are you supposed to sit? Well, usually there will be a friend who's in your classes, but that isn't always the case. People are talking to each other, and you're just standing there. The "popular kids" have their own assigned seats, not by the teacher but by their own intuition. My advice: pick a seat where you know you won't get into any trouble.

The seat you picked might not be the best in the world, but it's a seat and I'd take it while I could. Then the teacher introduces themselves to you. Looking at the way they've dressed or their expressions, you can tell how the year is going to go.

Now here comes the semi-embarrassing part: calling the roll out in front of everyone. Everyone isn't big on their names, and as a person who has a long name that is hard to pronounce, I completely understand what you might have to go through.

Here it comes: the teacher calls your name. Don't be embarrassed. Here is a word that will save you any kind of trouble. When the teacher says your name, say "Here," and be done. Nothing else has to be said, but that very simple word. If your name is like mine, and the teacher pronounces it wrong, there may be some laughter. Don't let people like that ruin your day. Just tell them how to pronounce it, and that's all you have to say.

After that class, you have to transition into another. Many people are trying to get to their classes, and not all of them have manners. If I've learned anything, it's to always have manners and say "Excuse me." Kids aren't always polite, and everyone knows that.

Let's just say someone pushes you and doesn't even say the magic words: "Excuse me." Unless they push you really hard and shove you out of the way, don't worry about it. Just don't let them. Yes, people talk in the halls and they walk as slow as molasses and you really want to push them out of the way. To avoid any kind of conflict, just resist the urge to do that. No one—I mean *nobody*—wants to make an enemy on the first day; not the best way to start off the school year.

Time has finally come to get the most complicated thing in school: your new locker. Kids think getting a locker and having to unlock it with that special code is difficult—*not really!* Remember that code, and keep it safe. When I mean safe, I'm talking about the most secure place that you'll remember to get it later. Once kids go on breaks, they forget their code, and if you put it in a safe place, you'll always have it with you.

Now if you're reading this, you're probably thinking, *There's more to middle school than the first day.*' Don't worry; we have a lot of more ground to cover about your future experience

Chapter 2

Cafeteria Disasters

I'm not a fan of eating lunch at school; sometimes the lunchroom doesn't have the best smells. Eating lunch on the first day can be tricky. Normally, people want to fit in and act like someone else. *Don't do that.* I'm here to tell you that eating alone is okay. Many kids do that at lunch, and they seem totally fine. Now I'm not saying just be alone *period* and isolated from everyone. Being alone eating lunch is perfectly fine. In my opinion, people strive more without having someone constantly on their back.

Right now, you're saying in your mind, *I don't want to sit alone.* It's okay. All you have to do is find someone who looks interesting, and try and make conversation. I will warn you about something: looks can be deceiving. What that means is someone who looks nice might not always be nice and friendly.

I want your first time in the cafeteria to be great. I can't say it will be all that great if you're not a fan of cafeteria food. Here's a big tip: pack your own lunch. I think you'll feel better eating food from your own house or food that you trust.

One kid from my elementary school threw up from eating the school lunch. I would hate for that to be you.

If you have friends from your old school, by all means, please sit with them. Chat, sit, and enjoy your lunch. This is one of the few breaks that you'll get during the day to just relax. Lunch is meant to be a fun time for everyone. Make sure you have an awesome time, and chill for a minute. Be sure to check your time, and keep yourself on a schedule.

Most importantly: just have fun, and enjoy your time in the cafeteria.

Chapter 3

Making New Friends

Making new friends can be difficult in middle school. If you have a problem with this, you're not alone. I struggled with making new friends as well. In fact, if making new friends was a grade, mine wouldn't be an A. I thought that people who were friends long ago need to stay friends forever. That's when I learned that people move on, and some just don't want to be your friend anymore.

Remember this: you never know who you can trust in this world. Some people are devious and untrustworthy. Of course, you can't really tell until you get to know them; just be careful. Kids can get their feelings hurt from other kids. I honestly don't want you to be that person.

Everyone is different. I'm here to help you in the friend category part of your middle school life. Say you're one of the shy types, and making new friends isn't really your strong suit. Again, I say that is totally fine.

Here's a tip: never be afraid to meet someone new.

Here's an example. Say you see someone who looks like they are friendly and would love to have a new friend. If you struggle in the area of talking to others and get nervous around them, it's fine.

Starting a conversation can be as simple as giving someone a nice compliment about their outfit. That can be hard too. Maybe the person you want to talk to dropped their pencil, or they are reading a book that you like too. Try and find your common interest with each other.

This doesn't just go for the girls; this is for the boys too. Maybe you're a girl who wants to be friends with this boy. Go right ahead, even though it might be a little harder talking to them. Or you're a boy trying to be this girl's friend. There is nothing wrong with having girl and boy best friends. It's actually really good. I have some myself; some have become such good friends that I call them brothers. They are not my real brothers, but it helps in establishing a great relationship with each other.

Interacting with others is important in your middle school life. It will not only make making new friends easier but also ensure that you have to interact with each other in class. Know that people might be just like you.

This is one of the hardest subjects I can talk about. Not everyone is good with speaking to others, and some people just don't want to. Being afraid is okay; I was afraid in sixth grade. It was a learning experience for me. Since then, I've become a totally different person. I'm happy about that. I hope that you make some good friends who will stick by your side no matter what and keep you happy. That's what real friends are for.

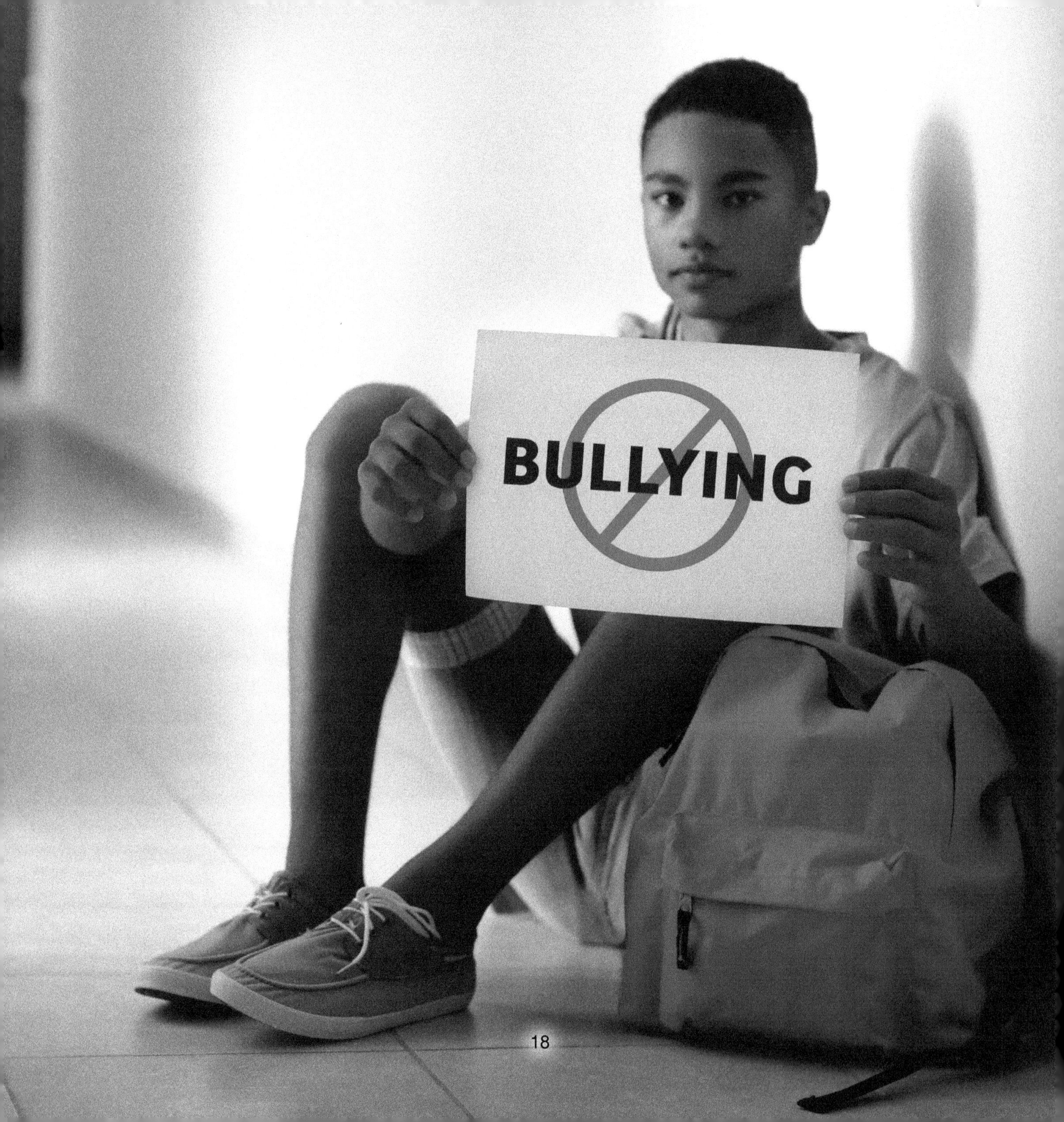
BULLYING

Chapter 4

Bullies

Kids are being bullied all around the world. This creates a lack of confidence. It's not okay to bully someone or to let someone bully you. I care about what happens to kids because we are the future. Bullies are not a cool thing. Staying and being in the crowd is not the best thing.

Take my suggestion: if you know you're a bully, and you're causing someone great pain and giving them hard times, *stop!*

Children have hard times already because they might be embarrassed about something. Everyone is different from each other. That's what makes us unique. If you're like me, you're not that big on your weight or height. I'm not short, but I've been called that since my middle school journey. Trust me when I say being called names isn't nice, and you can do something to stop that.

Ignore them! Once they realize that you've have ignored them, and it doesn't bother you anymore, they'll stop. You'll feel proud of yourself, and a flow of confidence will come your way.

Name-calling is considered nothing to what kids have really been through over the years. Kids have been pushed into lockers, slammed into walls, and punched in the face. Trust me when I say that's not even half of it. I've never been in that kind of situation, but I can understand what some of you have gone through. Someone who looks stronger than you and is bigger and older than you can make you hide in the shadows. To make you scared, they might say "Fight back" or "Take your best shot." Never give into peer pressure, there's a way to handle this situation.

Stand up for yourself! Now I don't want you to get suspended or expelled. I'm not trying to put any crazy ideas into your head. I mean, stand your ground. Tell them that you won't take any more of it, and it needs to stop. Bullies usually bully other kids because they're having a hard time in their life.

Sometimes maybe just asking why they pick on you and what's going on can solve the problem. You never know; you might end up having a new friend. Talking it out and working the situation out can stop kids in the future from being bullied.

If you're one of those people who would want to take them down and put a stop to it once and for all, listen: fight power with power! Take them out with their best game. Make sure you stop it once and for all.

Telling a teacher can also solve the problem. Just because a bully says that they will hurt you if you say anything doesn't make it true. Adults can work out the situation. Don't be afraid! Telling someone could end the problem quickly.

Allow me to share a situation that happened to me during my middle school experience. I thought my friends and I were fine, but one day, I was faced with an unexpected challenge. While we were eating and having a good time, one of the girls suggested we play Dare or Dare. Not Truth or Dare but Dare or Dare. Therefore, there is no way you can pick *truth*. My friends dared me to go up to a boy and say, "Do you like my sweater? I wore it just for you." I refused to do it because I did not want to and because it was stupid.

Then they dared me to do something else, and I refused again. They dared me to go hug someone, and I did. What happened? They all laughed at me behind my back. That got my attention. After that, they dared me to do other things, and I would not. The next day, when we were in the cafeteria, they wanted to play again. When it came to my turn, one of the girls said, "Okay, now it's *the wimp's* turn." That really hurt my feelings. I let her know that I was not a wimp, but she continued to call me that because I refused to do anymore dares. After that, the girls left me and walked away. They began treating me differently and leaving me out. It was at that point that I realized they were not the best people to hang out with. So I had to listen to and take my own advice. I found new people to talk to and to eat with during lunch.

Once I left that group and found more friendly people to hang out with, they came to my new group and talked to everyone except me. They purposely excluded me. That too was bullying, but I refused to give in to their treatment of me. I kept forging ahead with my new friendships. Once they saw that I was not going to do things their way, they left me alone. One of them sent me an ugly message on Instagram, but that was okay.

One strategy that I used that really helped me was something my mother taught me. She told me that I could not handle people, but God could. She told me to write their names on a piece of paper and insert it into the Bible at Psalm 37:1. That scripture says, "Fret not thyself because of evildoers, neither be thou envious against the workers of iniquity." You will not believe this. I did this on a Sunday, and on Monday afternoon, when I came from school, I had a message on Instagram from one of the girls apologizing for the way she behaved. God worked that one out for me. Actually, another girl apologized to me too the week before. Wow! You may not use the same method, but know that there is more than one way to skin a cat.

Just know that bullies have been a problem in this world for a long time. Kids stay at home, hurt themselves, and try and change because they don't feel like they belong.

You do belong in this world. You were put here for a reason. People like that are just trying to ruin your self-esteem. Be the best that you can be in this world.

Bullying needs to stop! This isn't something that should keep happening when our generation gets older. You never know where the future will take you. Someone who is brave enough to stop bullying could be the next hero for children all over the world.

Chapter 5

Gym Class

Kids can have problems in the physical area of their lives. Not everyone is athletic, strong, or good at sports. I can remember when we had to do the fitness test. I didn't get the highest on push-ups. Luckily, I had a chance to change that at the end of the year. The next time, I got the amount I was supposed to.

Youth nowadays are scared and don't want to go to gym class. I can't blame you because I'm not a big fan of gym class either. I participate because it's an easy A. To help you, I have some tips of my own.

1. Stop hiding during dodgeball!

It drives people nuts. Honestly, it doesn't help your case at all. I mean, find your inner strength. The strong kids who think like they've got everything going on might not have it together. Guess what, I've got a secret for you: you're strong too!

2. Bring fresh gym clothes!

The locker room is full of germs and diseases. Please don't make it worse by keeping your gym clothes dirty. If it isn't what we do in gym class, it's the locker room. I promise you it won't smell all that great. People don't take their gym clothes home when they need to. Bringing fresh gym clothes will save your nose some foul stenches.

3. Try at every exercise!

The pain will be over before you know it. Some gym teachers go over and beyond with exercising. From my point of view, it makes me want to scream. My friends and I just grunt when the teacher makes all of the classes do excruciating exercises. Other coaches just make us do a little bit, then build up at the end of the year. My advice: get it over with, and be done.

4. Get along with everyone!

Please just save time by doing this. Whether it's just running, or playing a game, try and get along. You don't have to like them. I'd even suggest putting on the fakest smile you've got. Not being mean, but it'll save so much time.

5.   No arguing with the teacher!

Even if you want to, just don't. Again, I say put on a fake smile. Teachers are adults; they deserve some respect. Plus, they know more than we do. Getting along will make you have a better day without an incident with your teacher. Yes, sometimes they seem like they're wrong because sometimes they are. Having a fake smile will make the day go by smoother.

*****

Gym class isn't everyone's game. These tips may help you at times in class. Remember, you are strong too. Never let anyone tell you differently.

Dear diARY

Chapter 6

Crushes

One day in your life, you're going to get married. Maybe you're one of those people who don't want to get married. Eventually, in middle school, you will have a crush, or someone will have a crush on you.

I have little experience in this category. All the guys I've liked have told me straight to my face that they don't like me. Sure, it was hard and hurt my feelings, but that's why they call them crushes. The same thing applies to guys too. If that girl doesn't see the real you, then she's not worth it.

Also, here's another tip: dressing to impress is stupid!

I tried doing that once, and boy was that dumb. Honestly, I'm trying to save you so much time. Crushes are the worst. I'm not saying don't have one or that it's not okay to like someone.

Be careful!

A little secret to help you out: people believe in people who believe in themselves. Trust me when I say people are fake. You can tell when people are fake. Don't be one of those people; you're better than that.

Now if you have a crush, they may like you back. Then maybe you really want to go out on a date. My advice: go for it. Walk up, and ask them with confidence. Now if the person says no, it's okay.

Leave and walk away. Those stupid excuses to say it's just a dare are totally lame. Unless it's really true, don't say it.

After the no answer, wait before you get all upset. I'm not saying it's not okay to cry. That is totally fine. Express your sadness in privacy and with friends. This is how you know if they are your true friends or not. They should be by your side all the time, especially in a situation like this. Friends are there to comfort you and make you feel joy and happiness.

Now, for a minute, let's say you got the yes answer. All I can tell you is to be happy, and hope everything goes great. I honestly would love to help you out on what to say and what to do. Thanks to me being the most unattractive person to boys, I can't.

I hope if you ever have a crush that this helps. I couldn't give you much, but I hope I gave you enough.

Advice from the Author

You are such a strong individual. People mess with you only to get in your head. My advice: ignore them. You know what you want to be. You have a plan for the future.

Middle school is like a roller coaster. It's a very wild ride. So many things can happen that you will surprise you.

Friends will be made and might hurt your feelings. Being alone is okay. Many days, I had to be alone, and it was actually nice to have some peace and quiet.

Feeling left out will make you sad, but you can handle it. I want your crazy middle school life to be wonderful or, if you're already in it, make it even better.

We are the future, you guys. Make the world a better place. Change the world. One day, I hope you become a very important individual. Not saying that you aren't already; I'm saying be a world changer.

You are smart, brave, and awesome! Keep being you, and never back down from what you know you can do. God put everyone on this earth for a reason. Discover your reason, and change the world

Always try your best at anything that comes toward you. Never be afraid. Everyone was put on this earth for a reason, whether you believe it or not. No matter what you think about yourself, you were made to do great things.

What I've learned in middle school is a lot. Still, today, in the eighth grade, I keep learning new things. I chose to write this book to help others out. I struggled in my first year, just trying to figure everything out. No one needs to have a hard time like I did.

I hope you got some great advice out of my book. Remember, guys, to keep God first because he will guide you. He is the best friend you will ever have.

About the Author

My name is Anastasia L. Douglas. I was born in Shreveport, Louisiana. I'm fourteen years old and attend Caddo Magnet High. During my seventh grade year of middle school at Caddo Middle Magnet, I wrote this book. During my time at CMM, I was a member of KCMM, a broadcasting club. As part of KCMM, I would broadcast current school news and respond to student issues by giving advice in a forum I called "Ask Ana." I was also in the National Junior Honor Society.

I attend the New Bethel Baptist Church in Williams, Louisiana—a little church in the country. Church is my happy place. On Sundays, I am always ready to go to church. I believe if you put *Him* first, *He* will guide you through the rest. Church isn't the only thing that makes me happy. In my free time, or anytime, I love dancing and jamming to music. Any tune that I like and can dance to, I start jamming.

My middle school experiences led me to write this book. I never thought I would be an author. I have always wanted to be a meteorologist or someone who makes a difference in the world. I hope, in the future, I can do something to make people happy and inspire them. Most importantly, I want to change the world for the better.

CPSIA information can be obtained
at www.ICGtesting.com
Printed in the USA
LVHW070510131120
671619LV00034B/493